Thanksgiving for Addie Mills means driving to a farm just outside the little town of Clear River, Nebraska with Dad and Grandma, and picking out the fattest turkey to go with the homemade cranberry sauce and creamed onions. But it also means much more than that, as Addie discovers this particular Thanksgiving in 1947.

Prompted by Miss Thompson's class discussion, Addie gets one of her brilliant ideas and sets out to make friends with a family enemy—mostly in the spirit of Thanksgiving. Enlisting the help of her best friend, Carla Mae, Addie carries out her secret plan with great success. Slowly the "enemy," old man Rhenquist, warms to Addie's bossy way, and is reluctantly persuaded to let her care for his horse.

But events soon take a dramatic turn, and Addie must face confusing feelings she has never known before. Addie's father is angry, and even more difficult to deal with than usual, but Addie's grandmother stands by her, as she always does when Addie needs her most. In the midst of her sadness, Addie finds that a life-long dream of hers has come true—but may slip through her fingers if she can't find a way to hold on to it.

First introduced as a CBS–TV Special, *The Thanksgiving Treasure* is a moving story of growing up, and of the real meaning of Thanksgiving.

The Thanksgiving Treasure

by Gail Rock

illustrated by Charles C. Gehm

Alfred A. Knopf New York

With acknowledgments to Alan Shayne and Eleanor Perry,
who did so much to bring "Addie" to life.

For Grandma and Dad

THIS IS A BORZOI BOOK PUBLISHED BY ALFRED A. KNOPF, INC.

 Published in the United States by Alfred A. Knopf, Inc., New York, and simultaneously in Canada by Random House of Canada Limited, Toronto. Distributed by Random House, Inc., New York. Designed by Elliot Epstein. Manufactured in the United States of America.

Library of Congress Cataloging in Publication Data

Rock, Gail. The Thanksgiving treasure.

SUMMARY: Addie's Thanksgiving gesture toward a crochety old man enriches both their lives.
[1. Thanksgiving Day—Fiction. 2. Friendship—Fiction. 3. Death—Fiction]
I. Title. PZ7.R587Th [Fic] 74-163 ISBN 0-394-82834-8
ISBN 0-394-92834-2 (lib. bdg.)

The Thanksgiving Treasure

Prologue

I'M AN ARTIST NOW, and I live and work in the city. At Thanksgiving time, I go to the supermarket and buy a turkey all wrapped in plastic. It's not much like the Thanksgivings I remember when I was growing up in a little Nebraska town in the 1940s.

Dad would drive out to a nearby farm, and my grandmother would have the farmer chase his turkeys around the yard a little, and she'd give them the once-over, and somehow choose the best one. The farmer would hold it down, and Grandma would poke the turkey in the chest a few times to be sure it was tender. Then there would be a lot of squawking and flying feathers, and we'd wrap the fresh turkey in newspaper, put it in the trunk of the car and drive home with it.

I remember those Thanksgivings, with the cranberries, creamed onions, squash and dressing, and one special one, when I found out what Thanksgiving really means.

Chapter One

IT ALL BEGAN on a Saturday morning in November, 1947. I was up early, and it was one of the few mornings of my life that I managed to get out of the house before breakfast. My grandmother had the idea that, if you didn't eat breakfast before you left the house in the morning, your whole body would fall apart by noon. I had visions of my bones going soft and my fingernails turning black and all of my long, brown hair dropping off on the ground behind me as I ran—all because I didn't eat my oatmeal before I went outside.

The only reason Grandma let me out that morning was that I had promised to be back in ten minutes. I wanted to run uptown to the post office and see if the special mail I was expecting had come. I ran the three blocks, burst through the post office door and stood gasping in front of our box, hoping to get the combination right the first time.

We had an old post office in Clear River, and the boxes were finicky. If you didn't get the dial turned to the exact place where the number clicked in, the box wouldn't open, and you'd have to start over again. Our combination was 3 to the right, 6½ to the left and 8½ to the right. I missed twice, and finally took off my gloves. I rubbed my hands together vigorously and tried to think of myself as a safecracker. I turned the dial delicately right, then left, then right again, and it finally clicked open.

There, with the other mail, was the pink "package" slip I had been waiting for. I ran to the window with it and asked Mrs. Dillon, the postmistress, if I could please have my package. She handed me a big manila envelope addressed to me, "Miss Adelaide Mills." Up in the corner was the return address, "Hollywood, USA." I ripped it open, and stood there looking at the photograph with an ecstatic expression on my face.

"Looks like something good," Mrs. Dillon said, smiling.

"It's terrific!" I said, and turned the photo so she could see it.

"My!" she said. "That's something!"

"I gotta go," I said, and tore out the door so I could get home within the promised ten minutes. Otherwise Grandma would be ready to send out the county sheriff to look for the starving child who hadn't eaten her oatmeal before leaving the house.

I barreled through the kitchen and dumped the other mail on the table in front of Dad and Grandma.

"It came, it came, it came!" I shouted.

"My Glory! What a racket!" said Grandma. "What came?"

"From Roy Rogers!"

"That all?" said Dad, going through the other mail. "Thought somebody left you a million dollars."

"This is worth more than money to me," I said. "Look at it!" I held it up for them to see.

"Sure looks like Roy Rogers," Dad said sarcastically. For some reason he was not thrilled by Roy Rogers.

"All dressed up in his fancy duds," said Grandma, admiring the photo. She understood because she had loved horses too, when she was a girl.

"And look at Trigger, Dad. Isn't he nifty?"

Dad looked skeptically at the photo. He was always hearing hints about horses from me, and he did his best to ignore them.

"It's autographed!" I said.

Dad squinted at it and read, "Keep smilin', Roy Rogers. Trigger, Smartest horse in the movies."

"Sit down and eat, Addie," said Grandma, giving me the quick once-over to see if I had suffered any ill effects from traveling six blocks without breakfast.

I propped the photo against the sugar bowl so I could look at it as I ate. "I'm going to put this on my bedroom wall where I can look at it first thing in the morning, when I wake up."

"It's your Grandmother's bedroom too," said Dad. "She might not like that cowboy on her wall."

"I don't mind," Grandma smiled. "I like Roy Rogers movies. They always have happy endings."

"Yeah," I said, "but Roy and Dale always spoil it at the end by acting icky with each other."

"That's a happy ending!" said Grandma.

"Yuck!" I replied emphatically, and finished my oatmeal in a hurry. Dad was putting on his coat and getting ready to go uptown for some gas.

"Dad, can you take my bike in the back of the pickup? I need air in my tires."

"Can't you just ride up and get it yourself? I've got a lot of errands to run."

"Dad, you *told* me never to ride on flat tires. It'll ruin them! And new bike tires are very expensive!" I could always get to Dad by mentioning money. It was the thing he seemed to think about most.

"OK, OK," he said, and I grabbed my coat and went out with him.

Dad was always acting irritated about one thing or another, but I knew that was just his nature. Actually I believed he enjoyed my company, even if he wouldn't admit it. Of course I did have quite a talent for annoying him, and sometimes it would flare up into a real battle. Grandma usually played referee and kept things from getting out of hand, and I was learning to watch my step around Dad and not provoke him.

Dad was the quiet type, and didn't talk much. He was tall and slender, and his dark hair was just beginning to gray at the temples, around his stern face. My mother had died more than ten years ago, just after I was born, and Grandma had come to live with us then. I knew Dad missed my mother a lot, and he hardly ever talked about her to me. Dad, Grandma and I had been a family ever since, and somehow our three generations managed to get along with each other.

I always enjoyed going for a ride with Dad in his old, red pickup truck. He kept it well tuned, doing all the work himself. He didn't think much of men who couldn't tune their own cars, and besides, he hated spending any money that wasn't absolutely necessary. He had owned the truck for a long time, but he was so careful with it that it was in better shape than many newer ones on the road.

It had been tractor-red when he first bought it, and he had taken it in for a paint job when it began to look shabby. The body shop had run out of red paint and had mixed in a bit of yellow and the truck had come out a bright, orangey-red flame color, almost sporty looking. Dad was furious with them, but he wasn't about to pay for another coat of paint, so he drove around in our bright red truck, looking embarrassed and hoping the color would fade quickly.

Neither of us was very good at talking about personal things with each other, and a rattling along the back roads gave us something to talk about . . . how high Olson's corn was or how low the Platte River was or whether those were Holsteins or Guernseys in the Allens' pasture or whether it looked like rain over to the West. It was always pleasant for both of us, chugging along in the old red truck.

We pulled in at Tony's Texaco Station, and Dad got the truck filled up while Tony checked my tires. I told him they had to be in good shape that day because Carla Mae Carter and I were going to ride out in the country to get fall bouquets, and it would be quite a trip. Tony said it was a good time for milkweed pods because all the fuzz hadn't blown out of them yet. I asked if he had seen any particularly good ones anywhere, and he said he thought there were some over toward the river. He put my bike into the back of the truck, and I hopped in, and Dad started to back out.

Just then a beat-up Model T was pulling in, and it bumped into the back of our pickup with a big bang. Dad got out, hopping mad, and so did the other driver, a gnarled, grubby old man who looked to be in his eighties. They seemed to recognize each other.

"Why the hell don't you watch where you're going?" Dad yelled.

"You backed into me!" shouted the old man. "You can't drive any better than you can dig a pond."

"I never dug a bad pond in my life," yelled my dad. "I ought to sue you for the money you owe me on it."

"That money will just about pay for the damage you done my car!" shouted the old man.

"Damage!" yelled my dad. "Hell, it looks better now than it did before you hit me." With that, he got back in and started to pull away.

I was embarrassed because Tony and all the guys in the station were watching and grinning their heads off.

"I'll get that money out of you one of these days!" Dad shouted at him as we drove off.

"Not in this life, you won't!" the old man shouted back.

"Is that old man Rehnquist?" I asked, as we drove off.

"Yeah," said Dad, angrily. "Stinking old goat."

I had guessed as much, because I had heard the story of Dad's feud with Rehnquist more than once around home. He was considered an archenemy of my family. He had once hired my father to dig a pond in his far pasture. My father went with his backhoe machine to do the job, and after it was finished, Rehnquist had only paid for half the job because the pond leaked.

My dad said it leaked because Rehnquist had insisted it be dug in the wrong place, and Rehnquist said it leaked because my father had done a bad job. Dad and Rehnquist never spoke again, until that morning at Tony's Texaco. The mere mention of Rehnquist in our house was a guarantee of name-calling by my father—something in which he seldom indulged. I, of course, believing my father to be right in all matters of business and tests of honesty, had no doubt that Rehnquist was the villain.

"Where does he live?" I asked, as we drove toward home.

"Way over on the other side of the Platte River bridge," said Dad. "End of nowhere. He lives like a hermit."

"A hermit? You mean he lives in a cave or a hut?"

"No, a run-down old farm. He won't let anyone come near the place. Doesn't talk to anyone."

"Oh," I said, thoughtfully. "Then he's a misanthrope."

"A what?"

"Misanthrope. We learned it in vocabulary a few days ago. That's a word for a person who hates people." I was always very good in vocabulary and tried to remember to use the new words we learned.

"Well, he hates people all right," said Dad. "I hear he keeps a shotgun to chase them away."

"Do you think he'd really shoot anybody?"

"Huh!" said Dad disgustedly. "He's just the type!"

Archenemy or not, I was more intrigued than ever with old man Rehnquist now that I had actually seen him.

Chapter Two

AS SOON AS I GOT HOME I started getting dressed for the day's ride. First, long underwear, wool socks and heavy wool pants; then a carefully planned combination of shirts and sweaters that would fit under my warm, blue wool jacket.

By this time in November, the Nebraska weather was getting snapping cold. The leaves were down off the trees, the sky was bright, fall blue, and the wind came whipping across the plains, carrying hints of snow from the tops of the Rockies to the West. It was no time to go out biking unprepared.

I had struggled into almost everything when Carla Mae arrived. She was so bundled up that my Grandmother hardly recognized her when she came in the front door.

"Zattie rettie?" Carla Mae asked.

"My land, Carla Mae," Grandma laughed. "Can't understand a word you're saying. Take off that muffler."

Grandma helped Carla Mae unwind part of the long, wool scarf that covered her chin and mouth.

"Is Addie ready?" Carla Mae repeated.

"I'm coming!" I screamed from the bedroom, and waddled out to the living room, dragging my boots and jacket with me.

Carla Mae and I giggled at the sight of each other.

"You look like a penguin," she snorted."

"Well, you look like a fat pig," I laughed back at her.

We both hopped and staggered around the living room, making horrible animal noises, while Grandma stood by shaking her head in amusement.

Carla Mae and I were best friends. She was eleven years old too, and lived in the house next door to me. Her family had moved there three years ago, in 1944, and we had been pals ever since. We were always at each other's houses, having lunch or dinner together and playing cards or building snowmen or just sitting around and giggling a lot. I loved going to Carla Mae's house because she had six younger brothers and sisters, and the place was always in a happy uproar.

My house was just the opposite: very quiet and orderly, with just Dad, Grandma and me. I think Carla Mae kind of liked the contrast at my house too. It was small, only a little four-room bungalow, but at our house we could play Monopoly without having a couple of babies crawling across the board upsetting the hotels and trying to eat all the money.

Our house seemed almost threadbare, compared to some others, but I knew it wasn't because we were poor. It was just that Dad believed in getting his money's worth out of everything. We had had the same kitchen linoleum and the old maple table and chairs since I could remember. And Grandma still cooked on an old, black, wood-burning range, while most other people in town had modern gas stoves. Our kitchen hadn't been modernized in any way. We still kept dishes in an old, brown hutch and had the kind of refrigerator with a motor chugging away on top.

The living room was spare too, with just one prickly brown horsehair sofa, Grandma's rocker, Dad's big easy chair and a little writing desk where we each had private drawers of belongings. A braided rag rug covered the living room linoleum, and lace curtains hung at the windows. Grandma was in charge of the "decorating," which consisted of a fancy cake plate propped up on the mantel, a cut-glass vase and a conch shell brought from Florida by a well-traveled aunt of mine. There were a few pictures on the wall: some New England snow scenes, a print of "The Angelus," and a fat baby picture of me which I found very embarrassing.

Our house was always neat as a pin, because Dad couldn't stand disorder, and no one was allowed to leave any personal belonging lying about out of place. I was glad no one was allowed to look in my private drawers in the writing desk, because they were a real jumble. That was how I did my part in keeping the rest of the house neat.

Carla Mae and I went over our check list one more time before we prepared for departure. We had newspapers and string for wrapping all the things up and tying them to the baskets of our bikes. My grandmother loaned us an old pair of scissors to cut with, and I took along my Girl Scout camping knife just in case. We would be gone most of the morning, so Grandma gave us oatmeal-raisin cookies tied up in wax paper for an energy snack.

I could always depend on Grandma to come up with something like cookies at the right time. She may have been a good sixty years older than I, but she understood me very well, and seemed to take pleasure in a lot of the things I found exciting. Since she was home all day, I actually spent more time with her than with Dad, and she influenced me in ways that I never realized until years later. She would sometimes disagree with me, but I never fought with her the way I did with Dad, and she was always there to help me over the rough spots. It was much easier for her to show affection than it was for Dad, and when she knew I was having a hard time getting through to him, she was always there to make up for it. Of course, that didn't mean that she let me get away with much. On the contrary.

"Now don't go riding too far out of town," said Grandma. "And stay off the highway. You remember what your dad told you."

"Yes, Grandma." I had heard it all before, and knew it by heart.

"And don't get into any poison ivy or poison sumac," she said.

"Yes, Grandma."

"And be sure and stay bundled up good."

"Yes, Grandma."

I knew very well I wasn't supposed to ride too far out of town, but Carla Mae and I always did it anyway when there was something really important at stake, and our fall bouquets were really important. This was an annual adventure for us, and we would bring back cattails, milkweed pods, bittersweet, thistles and red and gold leaves to make our special artistic arrangements. The most artistic bouquet would go to our sixth grade teacher, Miss Thompson, and the other two we would keep—one for my grandmother and one for Carla Mae's mother.

We took one last look at page 253 in our Girl Scout handbooks to make sure we could spot poison ivy, poison oak and poison sumac, and we were ready.

We pulled on our wool gloves, buttoned up our jackets, wrapped our mufflers around our faces and mumbled unintelligible good-byes to Grandma. I pulled a wool stocking cap down over my pigtails, made sure my glasses were on snugly, and we were off, clattering down the road toward the edge of town on our bicycles.

Carla Mae had been given a new bike the previous Christmas. Since she was the oldest, it would later be handed down to each of her six brothers and sisters in turn. Her bike was shiny green and had a headlight as well as a basket. We both had colored plastic streamers on our handlebars and planned to get fancy mud flaps as soon as we could save enough money. We already had them picked out and circled in the Sears & Roebuck catalogue. They were "fabulous white," with red reflectors. The crowning glory on both our bikes, though, was the raccoon tail we each had flying from our rear fender. We had saved for weeks to buy them and took extra good care of them, even brushing and combing them now and then.

But I was ashamed of my bike. I had wanted a bike for a long time, but my father didn't believe in just handing out that kind of money to people for no reason, so he advised me to save my allowance if I wanted one. I figured at that rate I would be thirty-five before I had a bike.

Meanwhile, my uncle in Omaha took pity on me and gave me an old bike that had been sitting in his garage. It hadn't been used for about fifteen years, but it worked very well. I was ashamed of it because it had skinny tires. Nobody had heard of "English" bikes or racing bikes in Clear River, Nebraska, in 1947, and everyone made fun of my weird bike. I had always noticed that it went faster than anyone else's with the same amount of effort, but that did not make up for the fact that it had embarrassing skinny tires. Besides, it was an ugly, dusty maroon color which Carla Mae and I called "icky brick." I hated it.

We set off in a northwest direction. Clear River was so small, a town of just 1500 people, that we only had to ride three blocks in any direction to get out of town. We soon came to the forbidden highway and wheeled out onto it without a second thought. If we were ever caught riding out here, we'd be in trouble at home, but we did it all the time anyway. We knew perfectly well how to ride on the left and watch for traffic, and there were certain times when we just knew that we were old enough and smart enough to go ahead and do things that our parents thought we shouldn't do.

Nebraska was probably one of the best places in the world to ride a bike. It was absolutely flat. That always irritated us in the winter when we wanted to go sledding—there was hardly even a slope around Clear River, let alone a hill, and the only shot you had on a sled was to run like crazy and belly-flop down on it. That hurt your stomach, and you didn't go very far anyway. But those flat plains were great for bike riding.

We loved speeding along the back roads on our bikes, and being out in the countryside gave us a great sense of freedom. There were few houses outside of town, just acres and acres of cornfields and wheatfields and grazing cattle. There were hardly any trees, except those that farmers had planted around their houses and for windbreaks along the sides of fields, so you could see for miles. Sound seemed to carry farther out in the country too. You could hear a dog barking a mile away, or a distant train whistle or the hum of big truck tires on another highway far to the North, and if you were lucky enough to ride past a meadow-lark in the summer wheat, he would fling sweet notes right in your ear. The larks had gone South by this time of the year though, and the cold wind stung our faces as we pedaled past the brown stubble of harvested corn.

One mile out on the highway was the Platte River, which was even more forbidden than the highway, and across the Platte River bridge was certainly the most forbidden place of all—old Walter Rehnquist's farm. I had an idea that we would find some big, fat cattails there, because they always grew in the marshy areas on riverside property like his. I headed straight for it, not telling Carla Mae where we were going.

Crossing the long, high bridge was scary, because it was old and narrow and full of holes, any one of which could send you sprawling off a bike. You had to get across quickly, because if cars came from both sides at once, there was just no room for a bike to get out of the way. There was a curve at the far end, so you couldn't see if cars were coming or not, and we got off our bikes and put our ears to the deck of the bridge to see if we could hear anything coming from up the road. We heard nothing, and we jumped on our bikes and rode across as fast as we could, lurching in and out of holes and hanging on for our lives. We tried not to look over the side of the bridge at the chunks of ice floating far below in the muddy water.

When we had gotten safely across, we stopped, panting with excitement and exertion. While we were standing there catching our breath, we heard a clopping noise on the bridge and looked back to see a classmate of ours, Billy Wild, coming toward us on his horse. Carla Mae was always teasing me about liking Billy. Sometimes he was OK, but a lot of the time he was disgusting, showing off his cowboy boots and his horse and yanking my pigtails and being a real pain.

"Hi there!" he called out.

"Here comes creepy Billy Wild—showing off," I whispered to Carla Mae.

"His horse looks like Roy Rogers' horse, doesn't it?" asked Carla Mae.

"No!" I said, impatiently. Carla Mae did not know a thing about horses. "Billy's horse is gray, and Trigger is a palomino."

"I mean its hair looks like Trigger's hair."

"That's not hair, dodo, that's a mane."

"Hi, what are you doing?" Billy asked as he rode up to us.

"That's for us to know and you to find out," I said in my coolest tone.

"Wanna ride, Carla Mae?" he asked.

"No, thanks," said Carla Mae.

"Why not?" asked Billy.

"I'm afraid of horses," she said.

"Afraid?" I said, disgusted with her, and stroked Cloudy's nose.

"C'mon, Carla Mae," he said. "I'll hold on to you."

"Not me," she said.

"You wanna ride, Addie?" Billy asked.

"Will you get off and let me ride by myself?"

"Nope."

"Why not?"

"You're a girl—you might fall off," he said, giving me a smug grin.

"Oh, drop dead!" I said, angrily. "Come on, Carla Mae, let's get out of here!"

We jumped on our bikes and started down the road.

"He's really cute," Carla Mae said, looking over at me to see my reaction.

"Cute!" I snorted. "He's a dodo and always will be!"

"He offered us a ride!"

"Sure," I said. "Because he wants to hang on to us and squeeze us. Yuck!"

Carla Mae laughed, and we rode on toward Rehnquist's.

Grandma had told me that Rehnquist had lived on his old farm alone for nearly fifteen years, since his wife had died, and that he never spoke to anyone and had no friends. The Rehnquists had never had any children, so he was still farming his place all alone. He had been selling off his land bit by bit, and had sold all his milk cows. He still had a few acres for growing vegetables, and in the summer he would come into town in his battered old car and sell corn and tomatoes and cucumbers and a few eggs to the grocery store.

As we rounded a bend in the road I saw the farm, and I knew it must be his place because his old Model T was in the yard. The big, old barn stood empty, with a broken hayrake rusting in the barnyard. Near the barn was his house, a boxy, white farmhouse with peeling paint and a big porch across the front with a creaky old porch swing.

I knew we shouldn't be there, but my curiosity had been aroused, and I wasn't going to be deterred by the mere threat of a horrible death.

Chapter Three

I STOPPED AND GOT OFF my bike, leaning it up against the fence a few yards down the road from his house.

"Why are we stopping here?" asked Carla Mae.

"Come with me," I said, starting to climb the fence.

"Why? Whose house is that?"

"Old Man Rehnquist's."

"Old Man Rehnquist's!" she gasped. "We can't go in there!" Carla Mae knew about Rehnquist's feud with my father, and being a loyal friend, she was perfectly willing to consider him her personal archenemy too.

"Who says we can't go in?" I asked, and went over the fence. "There's a little stream down there behind that barn, and I bet the cattails are great. I could see them from the road."

"Are you nuts? He'll come out and blast us to smithereens with his shotgun!"

"We'll jump on our bikes and beat it with the cattails if he comes out with his gun."

"If he comes out with a gun," said Carla Mae, "you can forget the darn cattails—I'll be running so fast you won't even see me."

"Chicken."

"Yeah? I bet you'll run even faster."

"We'll see," I said, pretending to be brave.

We quickly sneaked to a spot behind the barn where we couldn't be seen from the house. We were planning our next move when suddenly there was a noise from around the corner. We both flattened ourselves against the barn wall. I knew a shotgun would poke around the corner any second, and it would be all over. We waited a moment and nothing happened. I could feel my heart beating all the way through to my back.

I cautiously crept up to the corner of the barn and peeked around. Then I saw what the noise had been. There was a pinto horse there, eating some hay out of an open stall and bumping the door as she put her head in and out. I stepped softly toward her, and motioned Carla Mae to come along. When I got closer, I saw it was a mare with the prettiest face I had ever seen on a horse. She backed off when we approached, and I held out some hay to her. She looked at us for a moment, and then came slowly forward and nibbled the hay out of my hand.

"Addie, come on!" hissed Carla Mae.

"Wait a minute—I just want to get a good look at this horse. She's beautiful!"

"Oh, for gosh sakes! Horses aren't beautiful!"

Carla Mae was not much interested in horses, and she had no patience with my love for them. I would have happily given up any member of my family or any friend, including Carla Mae, to have a horse, but the mere mention of the word was enough to guarantee an argument from my father. He had grown up on a farm, and he saw nothing thrilling about a horse. He simply did not respond to my fantasies of riding at a gallop across the plains beside Roy Rogers and Dale Evans.

"Addie!" said Carla Mae. "Are we here to get cattails or not?"

"OK, OK. Just a minute!" I searched around in my pockets and finally found the wax paper-covered lump of oatmeal-raisin cookies. I took one and held it out to the horse. She gave it a delicate sniff and then chomped it down whole. I laughed and rubbed her nose. She looked very interested in the rest of the cookies, but I put them back in my pocket.

"Watch out, she might bite you!" said Carla Mae.

"Never," I said. "Look at her, she's so gentle. She's pretty too. I wonder what her name is? You know what she looks like? Marble cake, like my grandmother makes."

"Yeah," said Carla Mae. "She does, sorta. Will you come on!"

"OK. Good-bye, Marble Cake—oh, she's so dirty! She really needs grooming, and she's too fat."

"Addie!"

"All right, all right, I'm coming! Don't be so nervous!"

I reluctantly left the horse, and we sneaked up beyond the barn to the field where the cattails were waiting for us. I was thinking about the horse and wondering why the old man even kept her. He obviously didn't ride her, and I felt sorry for her, standing around alone all day with no exercise. I vowed I would come back and see her again somehow, and get to know her, even if Rehnquist was our archenemy.

When we got to the edge of the stream, we knew we had to work fast. The little marshy spot where the cattails grew was easily visible from Rehnquist's house, and we would have to get what we needed before he spotted us and came out and blasted us to Kingdom Come with his shotgun.

We worked in a hastily planned assembly line. I cut cattails with the old scissors, and as soon as I had a handful, I passed them quickly to Carla Mae. She wrapped newspaper around them for protection and tied them in a bundle. We worked frantically, and just as we were finishing up the second bundle, we heard the door of the house slam, and there he was.

His scraggly white hair was flying out from under his old cap with the ear flaps, and he was moving the best he could in his heavy wool jacket. His pants were tucked into the tops of high rubber boots. He had his shotgun in hand and was shouting something unintelligible at us.

"Addie!" screamed Carla Mae.

"He can't get us from that range with a shotgun," I shouted. "Do one more bunch!" I slashed clumsily at another clump of cattails and nearly threw them at Carla Mae. She fumbled with the string.

"Hurry!" I shouted at her, putting the scissors carefully back into my jacket pocket.

"Oh, I can't tie it!" she shrieked, and got up and started running back toward the fence and our bikes. I grabbed the other bundles of cattails and followed close on her heels. Marble Cake stopped chewing her hay for a moment and stared curiously at us as we streaked by her. We leaped over the fence, and when we got to our bikes, we threw the cattails into our baskets without waiting to lash them down.

Rehnquist was coming down off the porch toward us and leveling the gun in our direction.

"Git outta here!" he shouted in his raspy old voice. "Git offa my property, or I'll shoot ya!" He was so furious I was sure I could see foam at the corners of his mouth even from that distance.

"Go on, or I'll git the law on ya!" he bellowed, and shambled toward us as fast as he could on his gimpy old legs.

"Git!" he shouted again, and sighted through the gun and squinted at us, twisting up his grizzly old face.

We strained and grunted, pushing our bikes over the rutted road, and took off as fast as we could go. We pedaled standing up, pumping with such force that our bikes lurched back and forth under our hands and we could hardly steer. The loose cattails went flying out of my basket with every bump. As we rode away, I looked back, and Rehnquist was still standing out in his front yard, shouting into the wind and waving the gun.

About a half-mile down the road, we stopped to catch our breath and giggle with fear.

"Holy Moley," said Carla Mae breathlessly, hand over her heart. "That was close!"

"Oh, I wasn't scared," I bragged. "He probably can't even shoot straight."

"I don't want to find out," she said.

"Nuts, we lost half our cattails. Why didn't you tie up that last bunch?"

"I didn't feel like getting killed," she replied.

"Aw, we're practically bulletproof with all these clothes on," I said.

"Yeah?" said Carla Mae sarcastically. "Then how come you were riding even faster than I was, getting out of there?"

"I can't help it if my bike goes fast," I said, irritated. "It's these dumb, skinny tires."

"Ha!" she said, giving me a knowing look. For a best friend, Carla Mae could sometimes be very annoying.

Chapter Four

CARLA MAE AND I LOCATED the rest of the things we wanted, spotted both poison oak and poison sumac and successfully avoided them, and got home in time for a lunch of hot soup at my house.

Grandma was admiring all the things we had collected.

"My, where did you get those big cattails?"

"Oh, we know a place," I said.

"I hope you didn't go too far out," said Grandma, looking carefully at me.

Carla Mae and I became very interested in our soup, and in a few moments we were finished and went in to work on the living room floor making our three artistic arrangements. We were careful not to discuss any of the morning's adventure, because Grandma was very sharp, and I knew she'd catch on quickly that we had been up to something.

Grandma was seventy-three, and hard to fool. Whenever I forgot that and tried to put something over on her, I was sure to get caught.

Grandma always wore faded old house dresses and Indian moccasins and stockings with runs in them. With a dustcap on her hair and thick glasses sliding down her nose, she appeared to some people to be just a disheveled little old lady. Those who knew her knew better. She could be tender and loving, but she was also stubborn and domineering, and full of fire. And that fire had been applied to the seat of my pants more than once when I was younger.

Now that I was eleven and getting very tall, I was too big to spank. Grandma, after all, was only a shade over five feet. I had no doubt that she could have spanked me if she wanted to, because she was enormously strong, but she and Dad knew that at my age, the loss of my allowance caused me a lot more pain than a swat on the bottom.

So Carla Mae and I breathed not a word about Rehnquist or Marble Cake or the Platte River bridge or anything else that might give us away. Instead we busied ourselves stuffing various combinations of cattails, thistles, milkweed pods, leaves and bittersweet into three decorated glass jars.

"I want more bittersweet in this one," said Carla Mae. "My mother loves red."

"If you make it too red, it's going to look like a Christmas bouquet, not a fall bouquet." I considered myself the expert on artistic matters, since I planned to be an artist and live in a garret in Paris when I grew up.

"Well, then she can get double use out of it," replied Carla Mae. "She'll save it until Christmas." Carla Mae had a practical streak that sometimes clashed annoyingly with my romantic streak.

"The point is to make it look like fall . . . with lots of browns and golds, and just a bit of red for an accent."

"Well," Carla Mae said haughtily, "I don't have an accent."

"Oh, all right. Ruin yours if you want to, but we're going to make Miss Thompson's genuinely artistic. She has very good taste, and she'll know whether it's done right."

Carla Mae rolled her eyes in exasperation and jammed another big hunk of bittersweet into her bouquet.

The next morning, we carried the most artistic of our arrangements to school and presented it to Miss Thompson.

We all adored Miss Thompson. She was young and beautiful, and it was obvious to us that she was the best teacher in the school. She had also been our teacher the previous year in fifth grade. That had been her first teaching job, and she had liked us so much she had requested to move to the sixth grade with us the next year. Though it was unusual, the principal approved. This had won her our loyalty for life, but it didn't really make us behave a whole lot better.

She was most appreciative when Carla Mae and I took her our arrangement. I had designed a particularly artistic card with a turkey on it, and it read, "To Miss Thompson for Thanksgiving, from Adelaide Mills and Carla Mae Carter." Miss Thompson showed it to the whole class and announced that Carla Mae and I were both obviously very artistic, which is just what we wanted to hear. Creepy Billy Wild called me a teacher's pet, and I made the ugliest face I knew at him.

That morning in school we were going to get started on one of our class Thanksgiving projects. We had gone to the grocery store on Main Street and bought a big roll of white butcher paper, which we taped all along one side of the wall, covering the blackboard. Miss Thompson had selected the four best artists in the class—Billy, Carla Mae, Tanya Smithers and me—and we would draw a huge cornucopia with all kinds of food spilling out of it, and a scene of Pilgrims and Indians eating the first Thanksgiving dinner. Then the whole class would participate in painting the mural with watercolors.

While the rest of the class worked on other art assignments, Carla Mae, Billy, Tanya and I set to work drawing the cornucopia. Billy had brought a Burpee's seed catalogue from home, and he suggested we use it to get ideas for drawing the fruits and vegetables.

"That's cheating!" said Tanya.

"Oh, it is not," I replied. "All great artists use models to draw from."

"Well, I think we should freehand everything," sniffed Tanya.

"Well, what do *you* know?" asked Carla Mae. "Addie is the best artist in the class."

"Come on," said Billy impatiently. "Tanya can draw freehand, and the rest of us will use the catalogue."

Carla Mae and I set ourselves the task of drawing some bumpy squash out of the Burpee's catalogue, and Billy was doing a pineapple from a picture he had clipped out of the *Saturday Evening Post.*

Tanya came over and looked at our squash drawings.

"Ugly," she pronounced, in her best snobbish style.

"Well, squash are part of nature's bounty too," I said coldly.

"Oh, Tanya," said Carla Mae. "You're just jealous because all you can draw freehand are autumn leaves and apples. Admit it and draw from the catalogue like the rest of us."

Tanya stuck her nose in the air and went down to the other end of the mural and freehanded a few autumn leaves drifting around the side of the cornucopia.

None of us liked Tanya very well. She was always taking dancing lessons, and showing off about how talented she was. She was very snobbish because her father had a lot of money. He owned the big gravel pits at the edge of town and my father worked for Mr. Smithers, loading the gravel trucks with his big crane. When Tanya wanted to be really snobbish, she would hint about how her father was my father's boss and made a lot more money. We still were pals though, because Clear River was such a small town that you had to be more or less friends with everyone, otherwise there weren't enough people to go around. But I definitely considered Tanya my worst friend in the sixth grade.

We worked on our drawing for a while, then Miss Thompson called us all back to our seats for English period. In history period we had been studying the first Thanksgiving, and we had all been assigned to write essays on what we thought the Pilgrims had meant Thanksgiving to symbolize.

Miss Thompson called on Tanya first. "It symbolizes giving thanks," Tanya answered.

Everybody snickered at that, and Miss Thompson smiled.

"Well, yes, Tanya, but that's fairly obvious. Can anyone else take it further?"

"They were thankful for their bountiful harvest," I answered.

"Yes, Addie. And what else? Billy?"

"They were thankful because they made friends with the Indians."

"Yes," said Miss Thompson. "They had made friends with

some of the Indians. And can anyone tell me how the first Thanksgiving itself contributed to the friendship between the Pilgrims and the Indians?"

"The Pilgrims invited the Indians to dinner," Carla Mae answered. "And the Indians were glad to have a lot to eat."

"Yes," said Miss Thompson. "The Pilgrims did invite the Indians, but let's not forget that the Indians taught the Pilgrims how to raise a lot of their crops and trap the game, or the Pilgrims would have gone hungry. What did they hope to accomplish, then, by inviting the Indians to dinner?"

"They wanted to be better friends with them," said Billy.

"Right," said Miss Thompson. "They wanted to strengthen their friendship, and they invited some of the Indians who were their enemies so they would become friends and share each other's food and culture. So you see, Thanksgiving also symbolizes friendship."

"You mean we should invite our enemies to Thanksgiving dinner?" I asked.

Miss Thompson smiled. "Why, yes, I suppose that might be a good way of building a friendship with them."

The class went on with the discussion, but I never heard the rest of it. I was still thinking about what Miss Thompson had said . . . inviting enemies to dinner. I had a terrific idea.

Chapter Five

THAT NIGHT AT DINNER, I was careful to keep my elbows off the table and pass the butter before I was asked. I even sat up straight in my chair instead of slouching and squirming, which my dad probably thought was a miracle, but he did not comment on it.

This was all calculated to put him in a good mood after dinner, at which time I would approach him with my latest brilliant idea. I came up with a brilliant idea every now and then. They seldom impressed my father.

My most recent brainstorm had been to string a pulley clothesline between Carla Mae's house and ours so we could send messages back and forth on it. We didn't have a telephone in the house because Grandma said it was just a newfangled gadget and that if it rang, she would just have to answer it. I tried to explain that answering it was the whole idea, but got nowhere. Besides, Dad never spent any money that wasn't absolutely necessary. He figured that if somebody wanted to tell us something, they could darn well come right out and do it face to face, or write a letter where you could see it all set down in words. So we didn't have a telephone, or a pulley clothesline, to any of our frequently called upon neighbors.

This resulted in a lot of tramping back and forth by Carla

Mae and me until we had worn an ugly path across the lawn between our two houses. We were told to use the sidewalk, but we never did. Carla Mae's mother and my grandmother, both being avid gardeners, decided they would thwart this path-making by planting a row of hedges between the two houses. Rather than diverting us to the sidewalk and saving the lawn, this only challenged us to newer and greater heights—literally.

Now, instead of simply walking across the lawn, we ran and leaped across the hedge, landing with a thud on the other side. And now, instead of a mere trail across the lawn, there were great bare spots on either side of the hedge, where we took off and landed. The higher the hedge got, the harder we ran and the longer we leaped, so the lawn became more and more scarred. In the winter, we couldn't get a very speedy takeoff in the deep snow and often brushed the top of the hedge on the way over, breaking off brittle little branches, much to the dismay of Grandma and Mrs. Carter.

They had finally given up and left the hedge and the trail and the two bare spots, and just tried to look the other way. For that reason, I think Grandma had been almost in favor of my clothesline pulley idea, but Dad said it would make us look like a tenement in New York City, and that was the end of that. That defeat had come only a few weeks ago, but I figured he had forgotten about it by now, and I was ready to try my latest brilliant idea on him.

After dinner, when Grandma and I had finished the dishes, I got Dad to play checkers with me. He would often play games with me, and the thing I liked best was that he never pretended to lose. I hated it when grownups would "let" you win at games, because I always wanted to try and win on my own. Once in a while I could win from Dad, but not very often.

He sat in his big chair in the living room, and I sat on the floor, and we put the checkerboard between us on his footstool. Grandma sat in her rocker, doing some mending.

We always gathered in the living room after dinner, and usually Dad would read his paper and sometimes turn on the radio, and Grandma and I would busy ourselves with our own projects, trying not to disturb him. The big chair was always his, and if anyone else sat in it while he was out of the room, he would glare when he returned, and that person would jump up as if Dad were Papa Bear discovering Goldilocks. Grandma liked her old rocker, and that left me the prickly horsehair sofa with the crocheted doilies. That was fine with me, since I liked to spread out at whatever I was doing. Often I would end up on the floor, using the rag rug as my base. If things got too boring, I busied myself trying to count all the different fabrics braided into the rug. I once got to seventy-eight and lost track. I don't think I ever did finish it.

"Who's coming to our house for Thanksgiving?" I asked, as Dad studied his next move on the checkerboard..

"You know who's coming," Grandma said, looking at me quizzically. "Uncle Will and Aunt Nora and little Henry."

"Little Henry!" I said, making my worst face. "Yuck!"

"Now, stop that," said Grandma. "He's your own flesh and blood!"

"Can't we have people who aren't related to us?" I said, trying to be casual. "Like the Pilgrims invited the Indians?"

"Afraid we don't know any Indians," Dad said, laughing at his own awful joke.

I gave him a disgusted look. "I mean we could invite an enemy and make him into a friend."

"We don't have any enemies, Addie," said Grandma.

"Dad does," I said quietly, peeking at him to see his reaction.

"Who's that?" he asked, distracted by the move I had just made.

"Well," I said, "maybe he wouldn't be your enemy if we invited him to our Thanksgiving dinner."

"Who?" he asked again.

"Mr. Rehnquist."

He looked up, startled. "Where did you ever get a nutty idea like that? I wouldn't let him into the yard, let alone into the house!"

I plunged ahead with the speech I had prepared. "Miss Thompson said that Thanksgiving symbolizes friendship, and I just thought that it would be nice to have him here . . ."

"Well, think again before you come up with another damn fool idea like that!" he shouted.

"James!" said Grandma.

"Miss Thompson said . . ." I went on.

"I don't give a damn what Miss Thompson said!"

"James!" said Grandma again. "Your language!"

"That man cheated me out of hard-earned money," my father shouted, "And my daughter wants to invite him here to dinner!"

"But Miss Thompson said that Thanksgiving . . ."

"Tell Miss Thompson to have him for dinner then," he shouted. "Boiled! And don't you ever mention the name Rehnquist to me again!"

He had made a dumb move while he was busy yelling at me,

so I reached over and jumped three of his checkers and got one of mine into the king row. He took one look at what I had done and got up out of his chair.

"I don't want to play anymore," he said angrily, and left the room.

I looked at Grandma, and she just gave me a sympathetic smile and shook her head silently as if to say, "You should know better by now."

She was right. It was silly to have tried something that imaginative on Dad. I pondered it while I put the checkers away. I was thinking about Marble Cake too, and I got another brilliant idea. I would spring this one on Carla Mae. She was usually a lot more receptive to my brilliant ideas than Dad was.

Chapter Six

THE NEXT DAY IN SCHOOL, I plotted just the right moment to approach Carla Mae. I decided I would try her when we were working on the mural again at the end of the day. First we had to rehearse our special Thanksgiving radio play, which we would do for the grade school assembly the next day.

Several of us had done research in our history books about the first Thanksgiving, and had written the play together. When we were ready, the actors took their places behind a folding screen at the front of the classroom. Our "director," Joseph Tilton, sat back there with us, sound effects ready.

I was cast as Betsy, a Pilgrim woman; Cora Sue was Mrs. Carver; Jimmy Walsh was Deacon Carver; Billy Wild was Squanto the Indian and Tom Matthews had a dual role as the announcer and a sailor. When we were ready, Miss Thompson went to the old radio sitting on her desk and pretended to turn it on. As she tuned it in, we began our "broadcast":

> ANNOUNCER (in deep resonant voice): "From the heart of the busy metropolis of Clear River, Nebraska, crossroads of the world, we bring you (dramatically) 'Great Moments in History'! Today—'The First Thanksgiving.' The year is 1620; the place, somewhere in the Atlantic Ocean."

Joseph then made sound effects of a storm at sea by doing his impression of the wind whistling and by jiggling a big piece of cardboard to imitate thunder. That sent the class into a fit of giggles, and Miss Thompson had to quiet them down so we could get on with our broadcast.

Betsy (sounding sick): "Oh . . . this Mayflower is a terrible ship! I've been seasick for months! Where's your husband, Mrs. Carver?"
Mrs. Carver: "The Deacon is over there by the rail, praying for land."
Sailor: "Land Ho!"
Mrs. Carver: "His prayers have been answered!"
Betsy: "Oh, look! What a beautiful cape!"
Mrs. Carver: "And what a lot of cod there are in the water!"
Betsy: "Why don't we call it Cape Cod?"
Mrs. Carver: "Husband, how can we get ashore without getting wet?"
Deacon: "We can step out on that rock there. It looks pretty solid."
Betsy: "I think we should call it Plymouth Rock, after us, the Plymouth Company!"
Deacon: "Look, some of the natives have come to greet us!"

Joseph pounded on a tom-tom for the appropriate sound effects.

Squanto: "Greetings. My name is Squanto. I learned to speak your language from your English brothers who

came here many moons ago. I will help you to plant corn, and catch fish and trap beavers."
DEACON: "We were afraid the Indians would be our enemies."
SQUANTO: "I will show you how to make them your friends."
ANNOUNCER (deep voice): "One year later . . ."
DEACON: "Wife, it's one year since we landed at Plymouth Rock. Our crops have been bountiful. I think we should have a harvest festival."
MRS. CARVER: "Good husband, we women will bake corn bread and make puddings. We'll roast some ducks and have shellfish and wild berries. And let's play some of our games from England."
DEACON: "And we will give thanks to God."
BETSY: "I think we should call it Thanksgiving."
DEACON: "Good idea, Betsy. And I think we should invite Squanto and all the other Indians. Now I must go and shoot some turkeys."

Joseph then smacked a wood slat on the table top to imitate gunshots, and we all gobbled and croaked like shot turkeys. This created an uproar in the classroom, and it took Miss Thompson a few moments to restore order.

ANNOUNCER: "A few days later . . ."
DEACON: "Let us drink to Squanto and our other Indian friends and hope that this Thanksgiving will be celebrated for years to come, and always will be a symbol of friendship to the world."
ANNOUNCER: "Tune in again next month for another

exciting chapter from (dramatically) 'Great Moments in History'!"

The class applauded wildly, and we all stepped out from behind the screen and took our bows. Miss Thompson assured us that the whole assembly would like it equally well, and sent us off to work on the mural.

We were ready to start drawing the dinner scene with the Pilgrims and Indians.

"You do the women and the kids, and I'll do the men and the Indians," Billy Wild said to Carla Mae and Tanya and me.

"Why?" I asked, puzzled.

"Because you're girls," he answered smugly.

"Why should we paint women and kids just because we're girls?" I asked angrily. "Maybe we want to paint the Indians."

"Oh, Addie, I don't care," said Carla Mae, trying to avoid an argument.

"Well, I care!" I said, indignant. "If we're going to divide it up that way, why don't we get an Indian to paint the Indians and a . . . a turkey to paint the turkeys?"

"You're always starting an argument," said Billy, "and always trying to do boys' things!"

"Painting Indians is not a boys' thing!" I answered. "It's a painter's thing!"

Finally Miss Thompson intervened and simply divided the mural in half, and sent Tanya to work with Billy, while Carla Mae and I did the other half. As soon as the others were out of earshot, I got ready to present my brilliant idea to Carla Mae.

"Who's coming to your house for Thanksgiving dinner?" I asked her.

"Nobody," she said, then laughed. "We're all going to my grandmother's house. She's having the whole family."

"Good!" I said. "Then she won't mind one more."

"Who?" Carla Mae asked.

"I just got a terrific idea. You invite Mr. Rehnquist to have Thanksgiving dinner with you."

"Are you stark raving mad?" Carla Mae asked, looking at me incredulously.

"You know what Miss Thompson said about turning enemies into friends if you invite them to Thanksgiving dinner?"

"He's not *my* enemy!" she said. "He's yours. You invite him to *your* house!"

"I asked my father. He blew his top. So *you* have to invite Mr. Rehnquist."

"There are already nineteen people coming!" she said, exasperated.

"Great! Nobody will notice him."

"Forget it," she said. "There won't be enough chairs."

"Please!" I said. "He'll bring his own."

"Absolutely not!" said Carla Mae, and she went back to drawing.

I felt momentarily defeated, but I had an alternate brilliant idea all ready to go.

"There's only one alternative," I told her. "We'll have to take Thanksgiving dinner out there to him."

"You're crazy!" she said. "The only reason you want to go is to see that stupid horse."

"It is not!"

"Besides," she went on, "where are you going to get the dinner?"

"Swipe it."

"From where?"

"Right off the table," I said. "You can get some too, from your grandmother's."

"Oh, no!" Carla Mae said.

"Look," I said, trying to impress her with my logic, "it would be a lot easier for you. There's so many at your table the dog can come right up and snitch off the table and nobody notices. At my house there will just be six of us. I've got a much harder time of it."

"Well, count me out," said Carla Mae. "I'm not robbing food from the table, and I'm not going out there with you!"

"What kind of friend are you, anyway?"

"The kind that doesn't want to get killed," she said seriously.

"But just think how pleased he'll be when we knock on his door with a delicious dinner . . ."

"You have really cracked this time," she said, looking at me wide-eyed. "If you think I'm going out there and poke a turkey in his face so he can shoot us, you're keee-razy!"

"Oh, I'll do it then! I'll get all the food if you'll just help me carry it. He'd never really shoot at us anyway."

"How do you know?"

"As soon as we get there," I said, "you can hide behind a tree."

"What if he isn't home?" she asked, still searching for a way out.

"Where would he be? Nobody in their right mind would invite him out," I said, without thinking.

"You said it, I didn't," Carla Mae replied sarcastically.

"Besides, what if he's already cooked himself dinner . . . then he'll have two."

"Can you picture him cooking a turkey dinner? Anyway, he probably doesn't even know it's Thanksgiving. He probably doesn't even own a calendar, he's such a hermit."

She shook her head at me. "I'm not going!"

"What's the matter, are you chicken?"

"Cluck, cluck!" she said, shaking her head.

"You're my best friend, aren't you?"

She nodded her head.

"Well, what about our oath?" I asked.

She looked at me with a worried expression. I knew I had her trapped then, because Carla Mae and I had never gone back on our oath. I spit on my hand and held it out to her. She hesitated a moment, and then spit on her hand, and we shook, reciting our sacred oath in unison.

"Faithful friends through thick and thin,
If we lose or if we win,
Signed in blood and sealed with spit,
Our loyalty will never quit.
Cross your heart and hope to die,
Stick a needle in your eye.
Vow to keep the secret code,
Or turn into an ugly toad!"

Chapter Seven

BY THE TIME THANKSGIVING DAY ARRIVED, I was beginning to get very nervous. Carla Mae had refused to help steal food, so I would have to swipe a whole dinner for Rehnquist right out from under my family's noses.

I was prepared to wear my jeans to dinner, figuring that any food I could drag into my lap would be a bonus, and since I kept my jeans in a generally grubby condition, nobody would notice any spills on them. Grandma, however, announced that Thanksgiving was a dress-up occasion, and I was forced to wear a dress. I searched frantically through my closet for a dress with pockets big enough to hold a chunk of turkey wrapped in a napkin, but I had none, so I would have to be very careful.

I promised Grandma I would do all the cleaning up and serve the dessert, which surprised her, since I usually hated doing that job. However, I knew it would give me a good chance at completing my list of food.

Early in the afternoon, Uncle Will, Aunt Nora and little Henry arrived. Little Henry was poison as far as I was concerned, but I knew I had to be nice to him for the afternoon. He and I never did get along very well. He was only eight, and very spoiled. He cried whenever he didn't get what he wanted, and he was a terrible sissy. He was short and blond and had a pouty little face and whiny voice. I couldn't stand him. He had on a new suit, and everybody but me made a fuss over it.

Aunt Nora was OK, but she was a big, buxom woman, and was always hugging and squeezing and pinching cheeks, which drove me crazy. I never knew what to do when somebody pounced on me that way, and it embarrassed me. I also knew, though, that it would have hurt her feelings if I shied away from her affection, so I always stood like a slightly uncomfortable statue while she gave me lots of hugs and kisses.

"My, you're growing an inch a day!" she said, which only embarrassed me more. "You're going to be a long drink of water when you grow up!"

Uncle Will, who was my favorite, put his arm around my shoulder, and changed the subject to how I was doing in school. He always had a sense of when people were hurt or uncomfortable, and that was probably what made him such a good doctor. He was the quiet type when Aunt Nora was around, because she talked so much, but when you got him alone, he was good company.

We all gathered in the living room, and Grandma and Nora made frequent trips to the kitchen to see how the turkey was doing. The kitchen was too small to hold all six of us for dinner, so we had set up the kitchen table in the dining room and put in the extra leaves and put on the good table cloth and the good china and the good silver.

While we waited for the turkey, I took up a place at my usual end of the sofa and proceeded to wield the nutcracker for everyone who wanted nuts. Henry wanted to crack his own, and I finally gave in. He made a mess though, and I had to take the nutcracker away from him again and take charge, making sure that he didn't get any more nuts than absolutely necessary. He looked very pouty until dinner time, but I couldn't bother being annoyed with him. I kept thinking of my approaching challenge.

By the time dinner was ready I was so nervous I could hardly bend my knees to get into my chair. I sat stiffly at attention, never slouching or putting my elbows on the table so Dad would have no reason to look over at me. I passed everything before it was asked for, and I was especially thankful Aunt Nora was there. She talked nonstop, so there was never a lull in the conversation, and I had a better chance of getting things off my plate and into my lap without anybody hearing a big plop.

First I slid a piece of turkey into my lap while Uncle Will was busy telling Grandma how good the dressing was. I was just about ready to make the same move with half an acorn squash when I realized that my little cousin Henry was watching me from across the table. I froze, and then nonchalantly pretended to be interested in my creamed onions. I hadn't counted on Henry being a spy, but he looked like he was about to tell on me. He kept bragging about his new suit at the table, and I made faces at him to show how ugly I thought it was.

I sneaked a corn muffin out of the basket when Dad looked away, and Henry saw that too. He started to look under the table to see what I was doing with all the food, but I gave him a swift kick, and he stopped. I had just about everything that I could hide in my napkin by the time dinner ended, and I managed to get up from the table in a hunched position that hid it from view.

"What's the matter?" asked my father. "You got a stomach ache?"

"Uh . . . no!" I said, hurrying toward the kitchen. "I'm just in a hurry to clear the table."

Rotten little cousin Henry was right behind me, and insisted on helping. He followed me out to the kitchen, and hung his precious new suit jacket on a hook by the door, so he wouldn't get it dirty.

"What are you doing with that food?" he asked, as he saw me putting what I had swiped into wax paper and glass jars.

"What food?"

"I saw what you were doing," he said.

"If you saw me, what're you asking me for, you little pest?"

I went in to get more food off the table, and he followed, helping carry out some of the dishes. When we were back in the kitchen, he continued to watch me, standing there with the gravy boat in his hands.

"Why are you stealing all that food?" he asked. "Why can't you just ask Grandmother for it?"

"Why can't you just shut up?"

As I moved away from the sink, we bumped each other, and he spilled all the gravy on the floor. I was furious.

"Damn it!" I said. "Why don't you watch what you're doing?"

"Don't swear at me," he whined, "or I'll tell my mother."

"Stupid little dodo!" I said. "I needed that gravy!"

"Call me one more name, and I'll tell that you're stealing food."

"I dare you!" I said. "How would you like a fat lip?"

He ran to the door. "Mama!" he called.

"Henry!" I hissed. "Come here a minute . . ."

He came back.

"I've thought it over . . ." I said. "Instead of a fat lip, I'd rather give you three black eyes!"

"Well, you can't" he said, looking at me smugly. "So what will you give me?"

The little rat was blackmailing me. "What do you want?" I asked.

"That raccoon tail on your bike."

"Fat chance!" I exploded. "That cost me eight weeks allowance!"

"That's what I want."

"Absolutely not."

"Mama. . ." he started to call again.

"Hold it!" I said quickly. "I'll give you the streamers off my handle bars."

"Nope. I want the raccoon tail!"

"What about my collection of aggies?"

"Nope."

I didn't answer while I tried to figure a way out of it.

"Yes or no?" he asked.

He moved toward the door when I still didn't answer.

"Okay!" I said. "You win . . . Judas!"

He went back into the living room then, and I heard him tell his mother that I was going to give him my raccoon tail. She thought that was so nice of me, and told Grandma it was lovely the way Henry and I got along with each other. It really burned me up, and while they were talking, I went over to Henry's precious new jacket and carefully stuffed his pockets with mashed potatoes. It served him right.

I got through dessert, swiped a couple of pieces of pie in the kitchen, and met Carla Mae outside.

"Gad!" she said, "I thought I'd never get out of there. We had a million dishes to do!"

"That's easier than stealing a whole dinner right off the table," I said.

"Let's get going and get it over with," she said nervously. "I can't stay out too long, it's getting late."

"That's OK," I said, straight-faced. "It won't take him long to shoot us."

Carla Mae gave me a stricken look, then glared at me.

"Very funny," she said, and lurched off down the driveway on her bike.

"Oh, come on, I was just kidding. He won't shoot us if we go right up to the front door and knock like regular people. Everything will be OK. We'll just tell him we've brought him Thanksgiving dinner like the Pilgrims and the Indians."

"Yeah, sure," she said glumly. "That's what it'll say in the obituary column tomorrow."

Chapter Eight

WE PEDALED FURIOUSLY and got to Rehnquist's farm in record time, because we didn't want the food to get cold. We leaned our bikes against his front porch in just the right way so that we could make a quick getaway if necessary. We crept up onto the porch, Carla Mae hanging back a bit, and me trying to balance two bags of food.

"There's no light," she hissed. "He's not here. Let's go!"

"He's probably sitting in there in the dark!"

I kicked tentatively at the door and we waited.

The porch swing creaked in the wind, and we both spun around, half expecting to see him standing behind us with his shotgun.

I kicked again, louder, and I heard some movement inside. Suddenly, the door swung open, and there he stood in his rumpled old clothes, with a day's growth of scraggly whiskers. For a second there was absolute silence, as he stared at us, unbelieving, and we stared back at him, frightened to death. I was quick to notice that he didn't have his shotgun in his hand.

Finally I found my voice. "Happy Thanksgiving, Mr. Rehnquist!" I said, weakly.

"Get out!" he shouted. "Get off my porch!"

"But we've brought you a Thanksgiving feast . . ."

Suddenly he reached behind the door and pulled out his shotgun.

"Addie!" I heard Carla Mae gasp from somewhere behind me.

He leveled the gun at me. I was sure I could see all the way down inside the barrels and make out a couple of big red shells in there. But I was angry at him for being such a grouch and an ingrate, and nothing could stop me now.

"Go on!" I shouted. "Shoot me! I'm not afraid of you, you old misanthrope!"

"What?" he said. "The law is on my side. Law says people keep off my property!"

"I'm not hurting your darn old property."

"Go on!" he said. "Get out of here!"

I was about to lose the heavy bags, and he still had the gun leveled at me.

"Hurry up and shoot me," I said defiantly, "because I'm about to drop your dinner."

"What dinner?" he asked.

"I've brought you a Thanksgiving feast. I knew you wouldn't make a turkey, so I brought you some of ours."

"And candied sweet potatoes," said Carla Mae meekly, "and cranberry sauce . . ."

"And two pieces of pie!" I added.

"One pumpkin and one apple," said Carla Mae.

"What are you bringing me dinner for?" he said, slowly lowering the gun and squinting suspiciously at us.

"Because we're celebrating the spirit of Thanksgiving," I said. "The way the Pilgrims did with the Indians."

"We're the Pilgrims, and you're the Indian," said Carla Mae

idiotically, still hiding behind me. I elbowed her to shut up.

"Tell your folks I don't need no charity," he said irritably.

"My folks?" I said. "Are you kidding? If my father knew I was here, *he'd* probably shoot me. You're a mean old hermit who won't pay him."

"Who's your father?"

"He dug out your pond."

"You Jim Mills' kid?" he asked.

I nodded. "And I had to steal this dinner practically out of my father's mouth. Didn't I, Carla Mae?" She nodded. "Now that I've gone to all that trouble, the least you can do is eat it."

For a second, he seemed to be thinking all that over, and I took the opportunity to race past him and right into the house.

"Hey!" he shouted. "Come on back here . . .!" Before he could figure out what to do, Carla Mae had run past him too, and we were both inside his dingy old kitchen, dragging all the stuff out of the bags.

I had tried to guess what his house would look like inside, but it was even worse than I had imagined. It looked as though it hadn't really been cleaned since his wife had died fifteen years ago. There was an incredible clutter around the kitchen—dirty dishes, pots and pans, tools and parts of farm machinery, old newspapers, beat-up jackets and sweaters thrown here and there, peeling wallpaper, sagging cabinets and a rusty old pump in the sink. It was gloomy and scary, and later I realized it was sad to think of him living in that depressing place all alone.

There was an old concertina on the table, and as I was about to pick it up and move it, he grabbed it away from me.

"Hands off!" he said.

"Do you play that, Mr. Rehnquist?" I asked politely.

"No!" he said. "Why are you taking off your coats? I didn't ask you to stay."

"We want to serve you dinner," I said, and we grabbed a plate and some silverware from the pile on the sink and started laying out the dinner at his rickety old table.

"Dad-blamed kids!" he growled. "I said hands off. Go on, git outta here!" He put the gun down behind the door and came toward us.

Carla Mae backed away from the table a bit, but I could see he was looking with some interest at all the food, even while he was yelling at us, so I kept on dishing it out.

"I said git your hands off my stuff," he said, looking at me fiercely.

"This is all going to be cold if you don't sit down now and eat it," I said, using the same tone of voice my grandmother always used with me when I was late for supper.

"Don't boss me," he said, sounding almost pouty.

I kept on putting the food on his plate. He squinted down at it. "What's that yellow-looking stuff?" he asked.

"Creamed onions," I said brightly. "They're delicious!"

He tentatively poked a finger in the onions and licked it off. "Yeah," he said sounding annoyed. "Well . . . I suppose I'll have to eat up this junk to git the table cleared off." He glared at us again, then sat down, trying to look as uninterested as possible. I knew we had him hooked.

"Better get yourself a napkin," I said.

"Don't have any napkins!" he snapped.

"Not even paper?"

"No!" he said angrily.

"Well," I said, reaching for a dishtowel, "this will have to do."

"Hands off!" he shouted. "You're too bossy! I don't like bossy kids."

I shrugged and came back to the table, and Carla Mae and I sat down to watch him.

He looked over at us defiantly, as though he wasn't going to eat while we were watching, so we wouldn't have the satisfaction of getting the best of him. There was a long silence while he glared at us, and we stared back. He squirmed in his chair and grunted and looked down at the food and up at us and finally, he angrily grabbed a fork and jammed it into a hunk of turkey and wolfed it down as though he hadn't eaten in days. He glared at us the whole time, and we tried to look pleasant.

"How is it, Mr. Rehnquist?" I asked, after he had eaten a few bites.

"Not bad," he said grudgingly.

"That's my grandma's famous chestnut dressing."

"Not bad," he said again.

"There's not one store-bought thing in this dinner. I helped my grandma make that cranberry sauce. I grated the orange rind in it."

He looked at the jar and then stuck his finger right in and got a big glob and tasted it. Carla Mae and I gave each other a disgusted look.

"I had it before," he said. "My wife used to make it."

"Does it taste like oranges?" I asked.

"Yep. Your grandma's almost as good at cranberry sauce as my wife was," he said.

Then he reached into the sack to see if there was anything

else, and he found the lump of wax paper with a carrot and two sugar lumps in it.

"What's this?" he asked.

"Oh, don't eat that!" I said. "That's for Marble Cake!"

"Who?"

"Your horse."

"What do you know about my horse?" he asked, looking suspicious.

"Uh . . . we saw her . . ."

"When was that?"

"The other day," said Carla Mae without thinking. "When we were here." I gave her a kick under the table.

Rehnquist looked at us sharply. "You the two I caught sneaking around here the other day?"

"We had to sneak," I said. "We were afraid of you. We're not afraid of you now, though." I gave him a weak smile.

"Ya sure?" he asked.

"Yeah," I said, and Carla Mae nodded in agreement.

"Well, don't be so sure," he said. "I might shoot ya yet, if I catch you sneakin' around here again."

"We have no intention of sneaking, now that we're friends," I said. "We'll just come to your front door and knock."

"You stay away from my front door! Who says we're friends?"

"Well, aren't we?" I asked. "We brought you this terrific dinner, didn't we?"

"Why?" he asked.

"Well, because . . ."

"Because why?"

"Tell him again, Addie," said Carla Mae. "You know, about the spirit of Thanksgiving . . ."

I looked at him.

"I'm a pretty smart old gink," he said. "So don't fool around with me, sister. Tell me the truth!"

"I told you, it's the spirit of Thanksgiving, and . . . I was worried about your horse."

"You're worried about Treasure?" he said, looking at me curiously.

"Treasure?" I said. "Is that her name? That's nifty!"

"What are you worried about Treasure for?"

"She's in awful condition, Mr. Rehnquist. She's too fat. Someone ought to exercise her."

"I used to ride her when I had cows up to the north pasture," he said. "Now I don't have no cows, so she don't get rid."

"Well," I said, trying to sound nonchalant, "someone ought to care for her. Did you know that some people who have horses that need exercising actually pay someone to ride them?"

"Well," he said, squinting at me, "did you know that some people who got horses actually *get* paid for letting people ride them?"

"That sounds backward to me," I said, "but I'd be willing to exercise her for a fair trade in tadpoles and a couple of turtles out of your stream, and it seems to me that you'd be getting the better part of the deal . . . if you want to know the truth."

"Not so fast there," he said. "Turtles are worth money. They get as high as ten cents fer 'em down at the dime store!"

"That's because they have paintings on their backs," I answered quickly. "Yours are just plain."

"Why don't you get that father of yours to buy my horse," he said, "then you can exercise her whenever you want."

"My father won't buy me a horse," I said. "He won't even let me ride one."

"Your father won't let you ride a horse?" he asked, giving me a sly look.

"Nope."

"Okay," he said.

"Okay, what?"

"We got a deal," he said. "You can exercise her if you don't come around the house bothering me none."

"Honest?" I asked, not believing my ears.

"Yeah," he said.

To make sure he was going to stick to it, I spit on my hand and held it out for him to shake. Much to my surprise, he spit on his hand too and slapped it up against mine and shook. I drew back my hand, all wet and sticky, and tried not to make a face.

Then Carla Mae and I got up and cleared the table and gathered up the glass jars, because I knew Grandma would miss them. As we went out the door, Rehnquist said it was the best dinner he'd et in some time. He didn't exactly thank us, but we decided that's what he had meant to say.

Chapter Nine

I WENT BACK TO REHNQUIST's the very next afternoon. I leaned my bike up against the front porch, but didn't knock on the door, so he couldn't accuse me of disturbing him. I thought I saw him watching from behind the curtains as I went toward the barn.

Treasure was standing quietly in her stall, munching hay. I had brought her carrots and sugar again, and when I showed them to her, she came right to me. I talked to her, and let her get used to me a bit, then I found a brush and started to work on her. She was a little fidgety at first, but finally settled down and seemed to enjoy being groomed.

After that, I was out there almost every day after school and on weekend afternoons. I told my folks that I was going bike riding, which was partly true. Carla Mae came with me once or twice, but she wasn't much interested in horses, and was still a little afraid of Rehnquist. Eventually she stopped coming with me, but swore to keep my secret.

At first, Rehnquist had come out to the barn to see that I knew what I was doing, and then when he saw that I had the hang of it and wasn't going to kill myself, he left me pretty much on my own. I arranged a nice little tack room in the back of the barn, with all Treasure's things—brushes, liniment, saddle and bridle. Once Treasure was used to me, I saddled her up and walked her around behind the barn. As we got better acquainted, I rode her farther and faster, until we were galloping around like Roy Rogers himself.

Sometimes I would come into the barn and Rehnquist would be there, rubbing Treasure's nose and talking softly to her. When he saw me, he would look embarrassed and pretend that he had been talking to himself, and he'd suddenly get real busy with some chores somewhere else. I could tell the horse was a real pet to him, and that he missed riding her, now that he was too old.

I always took my sketch pad out to Rehnquist's, and would draw Treasure. One cold day I was sitting on the porch drawing, when I heard him playing his concertina inside. I wanted to go in and warm up, so I went up and knocked on the door. He grumped about how I was pestering him, but he let me in.

"You do play your concertina, don't you?" I said.

"No!" he said.

"I heard you!" I said, going over to the table where he had left it.

"Hands off!"

"I wasn't touching it."

"Yeah, well, don't!"

"You don't have to be so rude about it," I said.

He sat down with his face behind a newspaper and paid no more attention to me, so I went over and showed him my drawing of Treasure.

"What do you think?" I asked.

"Not bad."

I sat down in a chair facing him. "I'm going to draw a picture of you."

"Oh no you ain't!"

"Why not?"

"Go home!" he said, irritably.

"Just let me draw your picture!" I said, and started to sketch the outline of his face.

He squirmed away from me in his chair. "Stop that . . ."

"Sit still!" I ordered him.

"You're going to make some man a terrible wife someday!" he said angrily. "You're too bossy!"

"I'm not going to *be* a wife! I'm going to be a *painter!*" I kept on drawing.

"When you grow up, you'll get married," he said.

"Want to bet?"

"How will I know if I win?" he asked. "I won't be here when you grow up."

"Don't sit so stiffly. Relax!"

"I told you, I don't want you to draw my picture!"

"Now smile!"

"Smile?" he said. "What have I got to smile about? I've got a lot of hard work here, and nobody to help me. People cheat me, you come around pestering me. What have I got to smile about?"

"My father didn't cheat you!" I said, annoyed.

"Never mind about your father," he said, and hid his face behind his paper again.

"I can't see your face," I complained.

"Go on home. I got things to do!"

"Just let me finish this. I want to get the lines in your face right." I reached forward and pulled the newspaper away.

"Lines!" he said. "Wrinkles, you mean!"

"Well, wrinkles are interesting. My grandma has wrinkles. She says they're like a map . . . that all the things you've done in your life show on your face. I don't have any wrinkles because I haven't done anything yet." I looked at him more closely. "Next time I'll bring my paints. You have such blue eyes."

"Huh!" he said, raising the newspaper again. "Blue eyes!"

"Put down that newspaper, please."

"Boy, you're a bossy kid!" he said. "You remind me of a bossy little girl I once knew. She lived on the next farm when I was a boy. Pearlie Blake was her name. You're a lot like Pearlie."

He put his paper down and seemed to be thinking back for a moment.

"She was always bossing me around and getting both of us in trouble. I remember one time she was sassing her ma at the dinner table, and her ma sent her up to her room without any dessert. So Pearlie snitched a big plum out of the kitchen on the way up to her room. Then a few minutes later I come by outside her window and whistled up at her, and she was going to climb out the window. So she put the big plum in her mouth so she could use both hands to raise the window, and she just got her head out and *bam!* Down come the window right on her neck and she was stuck. She couldn't get no leverage to push the window up from inside, and she couldn't yell because the plum was stuck in her mouth."

He started to cackle at that, and I laughed too. It was the first time I had ever seen him even smile, let alone laugh.

"I about died laughing," he went on. "I finally went and got her ma, and she let her loose and give her a good spanking for it." He looked over at me. "So you better watch your step, sister."

"What happened to Pearlie?" I asked.

"I don't know," he said, sadly. "She moved away. She'd be old now, like me. Maybe she's dead."

He seemed to be lost in his memories, and didn't say any more, and neither did I. I kept on drawing, and he picked up his old concertina and began to play a sad little song I had never heard before. When he finished, he looked over at me and seemed to remember where he was. Before he could tell me to get out, I jumped up and showed him the sketch of him I had just done.

"How do you like it?"

"Ugly," he said.

"Would you like to have it?"

"What would I want with that?" he asked. "Go on home, you're wasting my time."

"OK, I'm going . . ."

"And don't forget to put Treasure in the barn and make sure she's got her feed . . ."

"I know, I know, I'll do it."

"Well, see that you don't forget . . . Pearlie!" he said.

As he went to open the door, I left the sketch of him behind on the kitchen table, where he'd be sure to find it.

The next time I was in the house, I saw the sketch hanging on the wall, all pasted down on a piece of cardboard, to keep it from getting wrinkled.

When he saw me looking at it, he looked embarrassed.

"Looks real good there," I said, feeling rather proud.

"Had ta get it out of the way somewhere," he said.

"Oh," I said. "I thought maybe you put it up there because you liked it."

"Smart-aleck kid," he mumbled. "Just like old Pearlie Blake."

"She must have been a lot of fun," I said, thinking of the story he had told me.

"Yep, that Pearlie was something," he laughed softly. "We used to have the best times together. I remember her dad had a big old pig that was Pearlie's pet. She used to ride him. She had an old wooden bucket that she took most of the staves out of and turned it upside down over the pig's back and sat on it like a saddle. And she'd get on that pig and ride all over the barnyard.

"One Sunday we just come back from Sunday School together . . . all dressed up, and Pearlie's ma told us to get changed into our old clothes before we played outdoors. Course old Pearlie never listened to her ma, so she just whistled at that pig and it come waddling out, and we both got on its back, and it took off running. Dumped us both right in the hog wallow. Oh, our clothes was covered! The worst thing you ever smelled.

"Pearlie's ma and pa came running, and I thought we was gonna be tanned for that, but when they saw us they busted out laughin' so hard they couldn't get mad. So Pearlie's pa just took us over to the horse tank and got a bucket and threw water on both of us till the slop was washed off. Then her ma pressed our clothes out dry. She never did tell my folks, or I'd a got tanned myself."

He looked at me for a moment. "You sure remind me of her," he said. "Smart-alecky as the day is long!" And he stomped on outdoors to do his chores.

After that I would sometimes sketch him doing things when

he was working around the house or the barn. I'd try to catch the line of his old body or the way he moved, and he would always shake his head and wonder aloud why I didn't get tired of that fool drawing. But he always wanted to see what I had done, and sometimes he would say that it about looked real, which I took to be a compliment, coming from him.

Meanwhile, I was going crazy trying to find enough time to sneak away from home and be with Treasure. I daydreamed that I could get Dad to buy her for me, but I knew it was just a dream. I made my usual big hints about horses at the dinner table every night. I wouldn't dare come right out and ask for a horse, but I thought talking about it—lots of mentions of Roy Rogers and Dale Evans and Trigger—might help. I always left my Roy Rogers comics lying around in conspicuous places, and cut out all the pictures of horses in the *Saturday Evening Post* and put them on my mirror.

My dad knew what I was up to and would make his own hints back, about how people who lived in town couldn't have horses unless they wanted a horse sleeping in bed with them, and then I would casually mention that Billy Wild kept his horse in Haskell's barn, which was very cheap. It was a rule of this game Dad and I seemed to be playing that neither of us ever mentioned directly that I wanted a horse. But I did ask for cowboy boots like Billy's.

"You never know when I might have a chance to ride somebody else's horse," I said, trying to sound practical. "At least I would be prepared with boots."

My father didn't seem impressed. "It's dangerous to go riding someone else's horse. You never know what might happen."

Grandma chimed in. "Cowboy boots will ruin your feet."

"Oh, Roy Rogers wears them all the time," I pointed out. "And his feet aren't ruined."

"You've got to wear good, sturdy oxfords until your feet stop growing," said Grandma.

"My gosh, I'll probably have to wear my oxfords to the senior prom when I'm in high school . . . just to make sure my darn feet don't get ruined!"

I got no further with any of my arguments, and I decided I should be happy that I had Treasure to take care of and ride once in a while. It never occurred to me that things might not go on forever just the way they were.

Chapter Ten

ONE COLD AFTERNOON I went out to Rehnquist's and found Treasure loose, grazing in the front yard. I couldn't imagine how she had got there, and I tied her to the porch rail and went to the door. I knocked, but got no answer and went on in. I called and heard Rehnquist answer from upstairs, but I could hardly make out what he was saying. I went up, and found him in bed, looking very pale.

"What's the matter, Mr. Rehnquist? Don't you feel well?"

"No," he said, weakly, "I'm fine . . . just resting."

"Do you have a cold? Want me to fix you a can of soup?"

"No, no . . . I ain't hungry."

"Are you sure you haven't got the flu?"

"No," he said. "I just got a bad case of old age . . . there's nothin' you can take for that."

"I found Treasure loose in the yard."

"Oh, yeah. I went to see to her, and I just got to feeling so tired I had to come in and lay down."

"That's OK, I'll go and take care of her now." I got up and started for the door.

"Sit down and talk to me for a minute," he said. "Treasure ain't going anyplace. You like that horse a lot, don't you?" I nodded and sat down in a chair near the bed.

"I like her too," he said. "She used to be the only thing I talked to around here before you came pestering me. I used to like horses the way you do, when I was a kid."

He seemed to be drifting off with his memories again, and I sat quietly and listened.

"That Pearlie Blake I told you about," he said. "Her father had a big old plow horse named Lucky. We used to take turns riding him. And in the winter, when he pulled the snowplow, Pearlie and me sat on the plow to make it heavy. Pearlie's father drove Lucky, and we'd go to all the farms around to push snow off the roads. It was cold . . . I can tell you that! But Pearlie and me would be all huddled up behind that steamy old horse, and we'd be snug as a bug. Every farmer would give Pearlie's father some hot cider to warm him up, and he'd give Pearlie and me a taste. The three of us would sing at the top of our lungs and laugh till we about split our sides. What a time! I think that bossy Pearlie was about the best friend I ever had."

He stopped for a moment and looked over at me.

"You're my friend too, ain't you?" He reached out for my hand, and I nodded and held his hand for a moment. It felt like it was on fire.

"You're so hot!" I said. "I think you have a fever."

I tried to feel his forehead. "Hands off!" he said, irritably.

"I'm going to get my Uncle Will," I said. "He's a doctor."

"I don't want no doctor poking around me. Sit down here and talk to me . . ."

"I promise I'll be right back," I said, and headed out the door.

"Come back here and talk to me," I heard him say as I left. "Don't you ever do anything you're told . . . bossy kid . . ."

I rode my bike as fast as I could back into town and went to

Uncle Will's office on Main Street. When I told him how Mr. Rehnquist had looked, he said we had better go right out there. He didn't even ask me how I had come to be at Rehnquist's. Uncle Will had that nice way of never bothering other people's privacy, and just getting the facts he needed, which was one reason folks liked him so much. I jumped into his car with him, and we drove quickly to Rehnquist's.

He went up to the bedroom, and I waited downstairs, sitting on the porch, talking to Treasure and finally going into the kitchen. I paced around and looked at my drawing of Mr. Rehnquist on the wall, and at his old concertina on the table. I wished Uncle Will would hurry and went back outside.

Finally he came out on the porch, pulling on his heavy coat and carrying his black doctor's bag.

"How is he?" I asked, going over to Uncle Will. "Can I go see him?"

"I'm afraid not," he said, sadly.

"How come?"

"He's dead, Addie," Uncle Will said gently.

"Dead?" I said, stunned. "But . . . but I never even said good-bye! I promised I'd be right back . . ."

"There wasn't anything I could do."

"Didn't he ask for me? Didn't he wonder where I was?"

"He was unconscious. I'm sorry, Addie."

I couldn't believe what had happened. I went slowly down off the porch and untied Treasure, and took her out to the barn. I didn't know what would happen to her now.

After I had taken care of Treasure, I went home and decided I had better tell the whole story to Grandma. I had learned by then that the best system was to tell Grandma first, and let her help break things to Dad.

She was down in the basement, doing the weekly laundry. It was always my job to help her put the clothes through the wringer and get them into the rinse tubs—first hot rinse and then cold rinse—then wring again and hang on the line with an apron-bag full of clothespins. Her old machine with the agitator made a chugging noise that we decided sounded like "choc-o-late, choc-o-late, choc-o-late," and we would often laugh and chant along with it while we did the washing.

Grandma would fish the steaming hot clothes out of the machine with a stick, then take hold of them with her bare hands and start them through the wringer. She never seemed to be burned by it, but as I took hold and pulled them through the other side, I could barely touch them for more than a second, and juggled them from hand to hand before I flipped them into the rinse tub.

Today, I didn't feel like laughing at the sound of the machine, and she sensed something was wrong. I began to tell her the whole story as we worked, and Grandma was surprised at all the things Carla Mae and I had done that we weren't supposed to do—riding so far out of town, going to Rehnquist's place and me riding a horse. She seemed pleased at the idea of our taking him dinner, though, and was particularly pleased that he had liked her whole-berry cranberry sauce with the grated orange rind.

"You know," she said. "If you'd asked me about that Thanksgiving dinner for Mr. Rehnquist, I'd have packed it myself and given it to you."

"I know, but I was afraid of what Dad would say."

"You were doing a good deed for a lonely old man."

"He said I'd make a terrible wife, because I was so bossy. He liked it though. He liked me making him sit still so I could draw his picture. I was going to paint him too, but I never got a chance. I didn't know he was going to die."

"We never know when that's going to happen, Addie."

"Mr. Rehnquist was nice to me. He let me ride Treasure. I think he was really a good person. I don't see why he had to die."

"We don't die because we're bad people, Addie," Grandma said. "Mr. Rehnquist was in his eighties. He lived out a full life. And look at me. I'm in my seventies—already outlived most of my friends and raised two families now."

I was startled by what she had said, and for the first time I realized just how old Grandma was.

"You're not going to die, are you?"

"Well," she laughed a little, "I sure don't feel like it right now, but someday I will. We all will."

"No, you won't!" I said angrily. "You've got to wait till I grow up! You'll live to be a hundred years old! I'll be a painter in Paris, France, and you'll come and live with me."

"What are you going to do with a hundred-year-old woman draggin' around after you?" Grandma asked.

"You could wear a beret," I said, picturing it all in my mind, "and we'd go to the top of the Eiffel Tower and drink wine."

"Now, don't talk nonsense," Grandma said, gently. "Besides, I wouldn't want to live to be a hundred."

"I don't want you to die!"

"We never want to lose the people we love," Grandma said quietly. "But we have to remember the good things about them, and keep those memories, and that's what you have to do with Mr. Rehnquist, just the way you remember the things I told you about your mother."

"But I never knew my mother," I said. "I've never known anybody who died before."

"I know, Addie, I know."

"I'm scared, Grandma. I just don't see why anyone has to die."

She came over to me and put her arms around me.

"Addie, I felt just that way when your Grandpa died. I thought I couldn't face another day knowing I wouldn't see him. And then one day, someone read something to me. It said, 'When people leave on a boat, you say, "There they go." But on the other side of the horizon, they're saying, "Here they come."' I thought . . . it must be something like that, and I was able to let Grandpa go."

I thought about what she said for a moment, and it seemed to make sense to me. I imagined Mr. Rehnquist meeting his old friend Pearlie Blake again, and what had happened didn't seem quite so terrible.

"Do you think I should go to Mr. Rehnquist's funeral?" I asked.

"I think that would be a very nice thing to do," said Grandma.

"I won't know what to do."

"Why, you don't have to do anything," she said. "Tell you what, I'll go with you."

"Oh, would you, Grandma? What if Dad finds out about it?"

"Never you mind," she said, hugging me close. "I'll take care of that."

"I can't believe I'll never see Mr. Rehnquist again."

"You made him happy," she said. "Like you've made me happy. Remember that, always remember that."

I cried then, and Grandma held me close.

Chapter Eleven

MR. REHNQUIST'S FUNERAL was that Saturday, and while Dad was busy doing some work on his pickup, Grandma and I quietly got dressed and left for the funeral parlor without telling him. I had on my best church dress, which was yellow with brown and white rickrack trim, my black patent leather Mary Janes with heavy white socks, and my hat, a navy blue sailor with a long ribbon down the back. Grandma wore her black dress she always wore to funerals, and her flat black hat with the pink rose on the side. I tied a brown ribbon on the fall bouquet I had made those weeks ago for Grandma and took it along for Mr. Rehnquist.

We set off down the street to Jensen's Funeral Home, and when we got there, we saw the hearse drawn up outside waiting. When we got inside, Mr. Jensen was there at the door to give us a Memorial Programme, and to help us sign the register. I wrote in my best penmanship, and noticed that there were no other names above ours. We were the first ones there, and Mr. Jensen's assistant ushered us in. Grandma and I sat in the fourth row of the little chapel. We never liked to sit right in the front row at church either, but we always sat close enough so Grandma could hear well.

This was the first funeral I had ever been to. I looked at the Memorial Programme and saw that it told when Mr. Rehnquist was born and the date he died, and it had a nice sketch of the funeral parlor on the front. I thought it was even better than I could have drawn myself. Mrs. Jensen was playing the organ, which was up at the front of the room with the casket. There was one bouquet of flowers on the casket.

We sat there for a while listening to Mrs. Jensen play the organ, and then Uncle Will came in and sat next to us. I thought it was nice of him to come since he hadn't even known Mr. Rehnquist until that last day. In a few moments, our preacher from the Presbyterian Church, Reverend Teasdale, came in and went to the lectern at the front of the chapel. He looked a little surprised when he saw me, and then he began to read from the Bible. I looked around and was startled to see that there was no one else there. Reverend Teasdale went right on through the service just as though we were a whole Sunday audience. Mrs. Jensen sang "The Old Rugged Cross," and then the Reverend read a list of nice things about Mr. Rehnquist that I had never heard of, and it was all over.

Mr. Jensen came in and ushered Grandma and Uncle Will and me past the casket. We stood there for a few moments and looked at him, and it wasn't scary the way I thought it would be at all. I tried to decide if I would say he "looked good" the way people always did when they came back from a funeral. He didn't look crabby, anyway, and I figured that was good.

Then Grandma and I went outside, and she said this was where you waited for the casket to come out. You had to do that to show respect. Soon Mr. Jensen, his assistant, Uncle Will and Reverend Teasdale carried the casket out and slid it into the hearse.

Mr. and Mrs. Jensen drove the hearse to the cemetery, and Reverend Teasdale took Uncle Will and Grandma and me. At the cemetery they moved the casket up to the hill where Mr. Rehnquist would be buried. We stood around the grave, and Reverend Teasdale said The Lord's Prayer and the Twenty-Third Psalm and then threw a handful of dirt over the casket. We stood there for a moment, and I wondered how it would feel to be asleep down in that dark hole with dirt over you.

Then Grandma and I put our fall bouquet, with Mr. Rehnquist's own cattails in it, on the casket, and we went home.

Grandma and I went in through the kitchen door, hoping we wouldn't run into Dad, but there he was, sitting at the kitchen table going over some bills.

"Where've you two been all dressed up like that?" he said, glancing at us.

I bolted for my bedroom door. "I've gotta go change out of my good dress," I said, and disappeared. I didn't want to be there for the fireworks I was afraid might follow.

"We've been downtown," I heard Grandma say, as I left the kitchen.

"Dressed like that?" asked Dad.

"Yes," said Grandma, "been to a funeral."

"Who was it this time?" said Dad, sounding as though she went to funerals every day.

"Would you like some coffee?" Grandma asked him, trying to change the subject.

"Yes, I would. Who was it?" he asked again.

"Walter Rehnquist," she said.

"Walter Rehnquist . . ." Dad said, absent-mindedly. Then suddenly he looked up. "Why did you go to Walter Rehnquist's funeral?"

"He didn't have any family, so we went," said Grandma, acting very casual.

"We?" said Dad, sounding surprised. "You mean Addie went with you?"

"Of course."

"Why did you take her?"

"He was a friend of hers," Grandma said quietly, "so naturally she wanted to pay her last respects."

I was listening carefully from behind my bedroom door as I changed. I figured this was it. I was right.

"A friend of hers?" Dad said incredulously. "What the hell are you talking about?"

"Calm down, James," said Grandma, and took him his coffee.

Dad was not about to calm down. "What do you mean, he was a friend of hers? She didn't even know him."

"Well, yes, she did, James," said Grandma, trying to keep calm.

"How?"

"She went out there to visit him a few times."

"Visit him?" roared Dad. "What the hell was she doing out there? Addie!" he shouted, getting up from the table. "Come in here!"

I yanked on my sweater and hesitantly went into the kitchen. "I didn't do anything wrong, Dad. I just took him some Thanksgiving dinner."

"You what?" he asked loudly.

"I knew he was your enemy, and Miss Thompson said we

should make friends out of our enemies, and you wouldn't let him come here . . ."

Grandma interrupted. "I think it was a very nice thing for her to do, James. Walter Rehnquist was a mighty lonely old man."

Dad stood there, looking from Grandma to me and back again. "That's the craziest thing I ever heard of," he said angrily. "You knew that old goat owed me money."

"He wasn't an old goat!" I said, angry myself.

"You knew I wouldn't want you going way out there!"

"Well," said Grandma, "I think it's a good thing she did. She found Mr. Rehnquist sick and got her Uncle Will. At least the old man didn't die alone."

Dad looked at me, and I could tell he was really furious. "I'm gonna lock that bike up for a month," he said, "and if you ever go that far out of town again, I'll take it away for good."

Just then, someone knocked on the door.

"Please don't make a fuss, James," Grandma said to Dad as she went to answer the door. "Addie's upset enough as it is."

"Think *I'm* not upset?" he said. "She could have gotten killed riding way out there."

Grandma opened the door, and there stood a tall, skinny man with blond hair and a sharp Adam's apple. He was dressed in a dark blue overcoat and was carrying a briefcase. He said he was the lawyer for the Rehnquist estate and wanted to speak to James and Addie Mills. I had no idea what was going on, but I was glad that Dad's tirade had been interrupted.

Mr. Burkhart told us that Mr. Rehnquist had left everything to his sister in Boise, Idaho. She had been too ill to come to the funeral, but Mr. Burkhart had come out to handle the estate. There was an addition to Rehnquist's will, in the form of a letter, which he wanted to read to us. We all sat down around the kitchen table, and he pulled the letter out of his big briefcase. He cleared his throat, which made his sharp Adam's apple plunge up and down, and started to read.

"I, Walter Rehnquist, being of sound mind, do write this letter, leaving to James Mills $234 as final payment for my pond, which I did not know was on a sandhole at the bottom."

I looked over at Dad, surprised, and he looked absolutely shocked.

Mr. Burkhart continued reading. "To Addie Mills, my faithful friend, I leave my horse, Treasure, together with the saddle, bridle and other such equipment. Signed, Walter Rehnquist."

I was numb.

"Wait a minute," said Dad, confused. "What's this about a horse?"

"Treasure," I mumbled, almost to myself. "He left me Treasure. Oh, Dad. Isn't that great?"

Dad looked at me and then at Grandma. "You didn't say anything about a horse."

Grandma looked a bit guilty. "Well, James, Mr. Rehnquist let Addie take care of his horse, and she rode it now and then. And isn't it wonderful that he left it to her?"

I could see from Dad's expression that he didn't think it was wonderful at all. "We'll talk about it later, Mother," he said ominously.

Mr. Burkhart, having no idea of the bomb he had just dropped in the lap of our family, went right on taking care of his business. "I'd appreciate it if you could go out and get the horse today, Mr. Mills, as there's no one at the farm to take care of it."

"I can't keep a horse," said Dad, sounding disgusted.

"Mr. Rehnquist left it to Addie, James, not to you," said Grandma.

"You know it's not possible for us to keep a horse!" he said to her. "We have no place to put it . . . we can't afford to feed it."

"If you don't want the animal," said Mr. Burkhart, "I'll have to make some arrangement to keep it until we can sell it, with the other farm equipment and household effects."

"Fine," said Dad. "You sell it . . ."

"She's not an 'it,' she's a 'she,' " I interrupted angrily.

". . . and send Addie the money care of our Post Office Box 72," Dad continued.

"I don't want the money. I want Treasure!" I said.

"Well," said Mr. Burkhart, "if you don't want the horse, it becomes part of the estate. The estate will sell the horse and keep the money."

"I don't follow you," said Dad, frowning. "That's ridiculous."

"It may seem ridiculous to you," said Mr. Burkhart, "but it was Mr. Rehnquist's intention to give your daughter the horse, not the money. Now, if you want to sell the horse after you get her, that's your business, but I can't do it for you."

"Oh, I can't be bothered selling a horse," said Dad. "Just keep the damn thing."

I was stunned at that decision, and frantically tried to think of a way to save the situation. Mr. Burkhart was getting up to leave. Suddenly I realized I had to appeal to my father's practical side.

"Wait a minute!" I said as Mr. Burkhart started for the door. "Would you please wait a minute?"

"Dad," I said, trying to sound conspiratorial, "Treasure's worth a lot of money. Why should somebody else get it? I'll help you sell her."

Grandma caught on immediately. "Addie's right, James. It'd just be throwing money away, and we could use it."

Dad looked a bit interested, and I was sure we had him hooked. Finally he spoke. "All right, Mr. Burkhart, we'll get the horse this afternoon. I don't know where we're going to keep it."

Mr. Burkhart left, and Dad told me to get my coat and that we would go get the horse right now. He went to get his coat.

Grandma and I looked at each other apprehensively.

"I think you'd better come too, Grandma," I said.

"Yes," she said. "I think I'd better."

Chapter Twelve

THE THREE OF US drove out to the Rehnquist farm, and I asked them to wait while I got something from the house. I went in and walked over to my drawing of Mr. Rehnquist, which was still hanging on the wall. I was pretty sure he wouldn't have minded if I kept it, and I took it down. I looked around the room one last time, and tried to fix it all in my mind so I could remember the good things about him, as Grandma had said. I went out then, and asked Dad to hold the picture for me while I went into the barn to get Treasure.

I could hear Dad and Grandma talking quietly outside as I saddled Treasure.

"James," said Grandma, "don't sell the horse."

"Don't you start on me, Mother. You know as well as I do we can't keep a horse."

"Maybe we could keep it in Haskell's barn," she said. "He wouldn't charge much."

"What's it going to eat? Table scraps?"

"I could manage to save a little out of the household money," said Grandma.

"If you can manage to save out of the household money, put it toward the coal bill."

"Well," said Grandma with a sigh, "I suppose you're right. I guess it's not the horse itself that matters, it's that she knows he left it to her—something of his. She began to love that old man, James."

"Really?" asked Dad, sounding surprised.

"Yes, I think she did," said Grandma. "You don't know your own daughter, James. She's got a lot of love to give."

Dad was silent for a while then, and I went on putting the tack on Treasure. I talked to her softly as I worked, and she would look at me now and then as though she were really trying hard to understand what I said.

"Mr. Rehnquist isn't here any more," I said to her. "And I'm going to take you to a new place for a while, where I can take good care of you. He wanted you to be with me, so it's all right.

"They were going to let you go up for auction," I told her. "And who knows what might have happened? Anybody could buy you at an auction! Someone who doesn't know anything about horses, or someone who wouldn't understand you. At least now I can have something to say about who buys you." She looked at me blankly, and I wished there were some way I could explain to her why she wasn't going to see her two best friends any more.

"Maybe we can sell you to somebody who lives nearby. Then I can come and visit you. Won't that be great?" I didn't even believe that myself. "Well, at least I'll make sure it's somebody who'll give you a good home." I hugged her around the neck, and she nuzzled me. I couldn't bear the idea of selling her.

When I had finished with the tack, I led her out of the barn. I didn't get on her, because I didn't know if Dad would let me ride her or not. He was leaning on the truck, staring up at Rehnquist's house and looking thoughtful.

When I came toward him, he came over and looked down at me, and patted Treasure on the nose.

"Would you like to ride her home, Addie?" he asked.

I didn't know how to thank him, so I just nodded.

Dad gave me a leg up on the horse and patted my hand. I think he knew then that Mr. Rehnquist really had been a friend of mine and that I was feeling both sad and happy at that moment, riding Treasure away from her old home for the last time. I trotted along behind the pickup, and we went slowly home.

Epilogue

MY DAD NEVER DID SELL Treasure. He talked about it a lot, but he kept putting it off. He said we might as well use the $234 Mr. Rehnquist had left him to take care of the horse, because he sure didn't want to use that old goat's money on himself. Then, on my next birthday, he gave me a pair of cowboy boots, and I knew that Treasure was really mine.

I did become an artist, and I even got to Paris, but by that time, Grandma was gone. Whenever I'd see something and think, "If only Grandma were here," I'd remember what she'd said about making her happy, and I knew that Clear River had been enough for her.

And now, not a Thanksgiving goes by that I don't think of that funny dinner in old Walter Rehnquist's kitchen, and how his friendship brought us all closer together and taught me what Thanksgiving really means.

ABOUT THE AUTHOR

Gail Rock grew up in Valley, Nebraska, a small town not unlike the Clear River of this book. After receiving a B.A. in Fine Arts from the University of Nebraska, she moved to New York and began a career in journalism. She has worked at *Women's Wear Daily* as a film and TV critic, and done freelance writing for newspapers and magazines, including *Ms.* magazine. Gail Rock currently writes TV scripts and is working on a motion picture screenplay.

The Thanksgiving Treasure and *The House Without a Christmas Tree*—another story about Addie Mills—were first introduced as CBS–TV Specials. They received much critical acclaim, and *The House Without a Christmas Tree* won a Christopher Award and an Emmy in 1973.